If You Give A Hors

Nathalie and James Pace

DEDICATION

To my children and my family N.P

To my children and my family   J.P

ACKNOWLEDGMENTS

To those that think they can and they actually do it! N.P

If you give a horse hot cocoa,

If you give a horse hot cocoa,
he will come and peek inside.
He will smell all of the chocolatey
goodness. What a wonderful surprise!

If you give a horse hot cocoa,
he will want to come in and stay.
He will rush in with his snow boots on.
He won't hesitate or delay!

The horse will want some ice,
because the cocoa is too hot.
You go grab as many ice cubes
as you can. He might want
a little, or he may want a lot.

The ice makes it too cold for him.
So he will want you to heat it up some more.
You run so fast to the microwave that cocoa
is spilling onto the floor!

He just can't wait to get his cocoa, as you bring him back his cup. He starts pointing with his boot. Now you see that he wants you to add some chocolate syrup!

You can really see that he loves chocolate syrup.
He is getting more and more eager
in his seat. You almost forgot, but there is
one last thing to add to complete this tasty treat.

You pile on the marshmallows until they spill.
Now there is nothing left to add.
Who knew a cup of hot cocoa could make a
horse this glad?

He first starts with the marshmallows.
The horse quickly eats them up!
He tries to drink every last drop of
cocoa and his nose gets stuck in the cup!

You bring him a straw. So he can finish his drink. He has no reason to be sad. By the smile on his face, you really do think, this is the best hot cocoa he's ever had!

He'll ask you for a second cup of cocoa.
And those donuts sitting there too!
With so many tasty treats all around, he
hardly knows what to do!

He nibbles on the donuts so swift and fast
that his golden mane dips into his glass.
Now you have one more thing on your list to do.
He now needs a bath and his hair shampooed!

He barely fits into the tub. He is happy that you are washing his hair. There are bubbles all around and he loves the suds. Water is spilling everywhere.

Now the horse is all clean, but he is still wet. So you will need to dry his hair. You grab a seat and your blow dryer too. He gets startled from the sound of the air!

He is all dry now but on his face there is a frown. His hair is flying high. He doesn't seem too pleased with this. You can tell by the look in his eyes.

You grab a comb and a stool to style his hair.
He likes the way it looks this time.
The horse is just smiling from ear to ear. So
you know everything is fine.

You go back into the kitchen. He is hungry for donuts again. He will ask you for some more hot cocoa too.

After all of this he seems worn out. What more could he want to do? He has played all day and even had a bath. His stomach is a little stuffed too. The horse looks exhausted and you let out a big yawn. He is getting tired and so are you!

Now it's off to bed you go. Your blanket and cover are tucked in tight. A day filled with fun and hot cocoa, is always a recipe for a good night!

The End

Made in the USA
Las Vegas, NV
02 August 2021